A SMALL THING FOR
YOLANDA

Jan Edwards

Jan Edwards is a UK author with several novels and many short stories in horror, fantasy, mainstream and crime fiction publications, including *The Mammoth Book of Folk Horror* and several volumes of the *MX Books of New Sherlock Holmes Stories*. Jan is an editor with the award-winning Alchemy Press (including *The Alchemy Press Book of Horrors volumes 1 and 2*.

She is a recipient of the Karl Edward Wagner Award (from the British Fantasy Society) and has also won the Arnold Bennett Book Prize for *Winter Downs* – the first in her World War Two crime series *The Bunch Courtney Investigations*. The second volume, *In Her Defence*, is also available. The third, *Listed Dead*, is on its way.

https://janedwardsblog.wordpress.com/

A SMALL THING FOR
YOLANDA

Jan Edwards

The Alchemy Press

First printing, 2018, Lycopolis Press
Second printing, 2020, Alchemy Press

ISBN 978-1-911034-10-0

Published by The Alchemy Press
www.alchemypress.co.uk

A SMALL THING FOR YOLANDA

The buildings were tall enough to imprison the street's darker recesses in a perpetual twilight, and packed close enough to echo the click-clack of her evening shoes on rough cobbles. The noise reverberated up between soot-stained stone into the blue skies beyond, almost but not quite disguising the scuff of softer soles trailing her from the shadows.

Laetitia Toureaux paused, not for the first time since leaving her apartment, to glance behind her. She was not a woman given to anxiousness or to nerves. She travelled often on le Métro to her beloved bal Musettes, and home again on the darkest of nights, and had never feared for her safety. Yet the impression she had of being followed ever since leaving her apartment on rue Pierre Bayle was raising the hairs on her neck. She had not sighted anyone tailing her, though she was quite expert at spotting those by now, yet had not shaken the sensation through two train changes. She rubbed at her bare arms and concentrated on the instinct that urged her to flight, trying to pinpoint the sources of her unease and failing yet again. Her natural caution was rapidly giving way to irritation.

Striations of summer traversed the passage at regular intervals, cutting between the stone buildings that crowded and jostled her from either side. A broad slant of light marked the end of a block and provided her with a perfect spot to assess her surroundings. She made a show of rooting out her compact and held it up at eye level, dabbing at her face with the velveteen applicator, whilst angling the mirror this way and that to inspect the alley. Bravado, she knew, but if she had a pursuer, and that was a big if, then let them know they were not as good as they thought they were, that she knew all about them.

Fifty metres behind her, two widows, clad in their black weeds from head to shabby toes, stood in the doorway of an apartment building exchanging woes at an excitable pace. Concierges, she supposed, bemoaning the short comings of their tenants, as was their habit. A large mangy street cur rose from the doorway where it had been resting and trotted past them, along the gutter. It detoured to piss against a door post, adding its own pungency to the warm foetid atmosphere. One of the women swung at it with her broom and was duly ignored. And all under the watchful glare of a large blue Persian cat perched on the sill of a second-floor apartment, its tail curling and uncurling in irritation at the disturbance to its sleep.

There was nothing new to the scene, nothing Laetitia had not already noted in passing, nothing to hint at anything undesirable trailing in her wake. She freshened her lipstick, deepening its hue to the striking cherry red of its name, and primped her dark hair into shape, before snapping the compact shut and continuing to the end of the passage into rue Le Pelletier and the relative safety of the Agence Rouff.

On the first turn on the stair she halted, peering down

into the vestibule for any sign of her shadow, but the street door remained closed. She continued to the landing, puzzled by that sense of surveillance nagging at her but certain as she could now be that she was wrong. Her only currently active case was at the wax factory, monitoring communist agitators for the factory's paranoid shareholders. She snorted and shook her head. The girls working there might talk big but none of them would risk their jobs by summoning the courage of their convictions, and acting against her, supposing they even suspected her, which she seriously doubted.

Laetitia hurried up the last few steps and on toward the dark wood door where *Georges Rouffignac – Agence Rouff* was emblazoned in gold script across its reeded-glass panel. The reception office behind it was plain and functional. Three small armchairs surrounded a coffee table on which lay the day's newspapers. An uncluttered wood desk next to the door made a suitable checkpoint for Rouffignac's guardian, Janine Guilleme – every bit as efficient as her dark suit and crisp white blouse hinted. Janine herself was making coffee over a small electric ring, filling the space with its dark-brown aroma. She turned to smile at Laetitia. "Good evening, Madame," she said and crossed to her desk to press the intercom. "Madame Toureaux has arrived, Sir."

"Good. Send her in and then you may go, Janine. It is getting late."

"Thank you, Sir. Go through, Madame. He's expecting you."

"Thank you, Janine. Give my regards to your daughter."

"I shall, Madame. Bonsoir."

Laetitia smiled to herself. Janine was a good friend of her mother, but never once permitted that to impinge on office hours. She patted Janine's shoulder as she passed and composed herself before pushing through to Georges Rouffignac's inner sanctum, with head high and swaying, with heels in line with toes, as the best modelling school had taught.

This was a far larger room with red Turkish rugs covering the space between the door and a vast mahogany desk sitting squarely in front of the window, a position that threw the desk's occupant into silhouette against the brightness of an early summer evening. She had an idea that Georges watched far too many American movies.

"Georges," she said. "You left me a message. What is so urgent you can ruin my one night to myself?"

"And good afternoon to you too, Laetitia. Come. Sit. I have a job for you and yes, it is most urgent."

"Must it be tonight? I promised my brother I would meet him and his friends."

"So meet him tomorrow night. An evening of dancing and champagne is hardly honest toil. You will still have a wonderful time but now it will all be on expenses. I shall make it be worth your while – and it's such a small thing for Yolanda."

The notion hung amidst air thick with stale smoke. Laetitia Toureaux was not afraid to contradict her boss, not in so many words, but her alter ego, Yolanda, was not brought into the open without good cause. The mention of that name was like the flipping of a switch. When she tried to examine this for herself she thought perhaps it was a cliché, but inhabiting her other self as completely as any actor at the Cinema de Paris was necessary, especially on those occasions when she might flip from one to the other on a daily or even hourly basis.

Laetitia, the widow woman earning her daily bread in the factory, vanished where she sat and Yolanda came fully formed to the party; deep, dark and mysterious. Yolanda reached for her cigarette case and took time in selecting a Gittane over Pariesienne before inserting it into the ebony holder. "So say you. Sitting there behind your desk, it is all so very easy." She counted to two, holder held between her lips, yet the expected light was not proffered.

If Georges Rouffignac was aware of the transformation taking place he gave no indication. He only took a drink from his demi tasse and carefully wiped each side of his neat moustache before adjusting his heavy-framed glasses to glower at her. He was a fleshy man, handsome once but too fond of lunches with Commissioner Badin to avoid his waistline spreading a little too far for comfort. He also knew far too much about Laetitia/Yolanda to fall for her charm – though she could not resist the challenge in trying.

"Who is this job for?" She lit her own cigarette and inhaled its aromatic smoke, letting the cloud plume above her head, before sitting back to view him through narrowed eyes. She had worked for Georges often but she did not completely trust him. Yet the money was always good and the excitement a distraction from widowhood and the dull aching loss of her husband. Even her paltry wage to be had from the wax factory was part of the game. A way, if not to forget, then at least to become lost in the moment.

She patted her dark curls that were cut and waved in Jean Harlow fashion and wondered briefly if platinum blonde would be to her advantage in her Yolanda persona. Jules had adored his raven-haired Italian wife Laetitia, but it was Yolanda who paid the bills, and it was in the role of Yolanda that she became aware Rouffignac was still talking.

"An … official department," he said.

"Sûreté?" she asked. "Or Gendarmerie?"

Georges avoided her gaze and shrugged. His evasion spoke of higher things and that pleased her in a perverse fashion. She had worked for shadows on several occasions and the prospect was enthralling. "Then who?" Yolanda flicked an imaginary speck from her linen skirt and smoothed the tiny creases from her thigh and slender waist and smiled to herself; she knew Rouffignac would be watching her every move, whatever he professed. She also knew he was not the only one doing so. The sounds from the office's further door were small, but her hearing, as well as her other four, and occasionally five, senses were excellent. She gestured vaguely. "Who are they, Georges? I am entitled to know."

"Better you know little of them," he growled.

"Better they come and tell me for themselves." Yolanda tapped her cigarette over a brimming ash tray, though it barely needed it, and raised her chin along with her voice. "You needn't skulk in the cloakroom on my account, boys. It's hardly sanitary and completely unnecessary." Silent expectation stretched out its limbs like a newly wakened cat. "Oh really." Yolanda uncrossed her legs and shimmied across to the door. She brought her quellazaire to scarlet lips and inhaled deeply before laying her hand on the cracked pitted handle and throwing the door open. "Entrée."

"Miss Toureaux." The older of the two men inclined his head as he passed her. He was close to passing his prime, though Yolanda guessed he had not realised it as yet. Carefully manicured, was her immediate impression – carefully *and* expensively manicured. Middle height with the build of a habitual tennis player. He passed a hand across his dark hair, preening under her attention. He was greying at the temples and, she thought, it was probably further from his brow than he might have wished as he eyed her up and down through calculating eyes. Here was a man who felt sure a woman such as she could not fail to be impressed by his air. She was equally certain her own charms would have him eating from her hand, should she so wish.

The second appeared younger but only on casual inspection. His was a strange face, wedge shaped and angular at every turn, with a long-pointed nose flaring expressively beneath her scrutiny. His freckled cheeks were just a shade off sunken and were framed by long sideburns. His silky brown hair was long enough to curl from beneath his butcher-boy cap almost to his upturned collar. But the feature that struck her most was his eyes: overlarge in such a gaunt face, and when they met hers she noted their colour – one hazel and the other green – which gave her pause for thought. They were not the eyes of some gauche pup. He was not classically handsome yet was possessed of a powerful attraction and she might have made a play for him had it not been for the way he appraised her in return.

He acknowledged her stare with another flaring of his

nostrils and Yolanda could not decide if it indicated complete disdain or some kind of fetish. She had been the object of both and it made little or no difference to her how she was regarded so long as she had control over it, and experience told her that she had the advantage over these agents. They would not be here unless they required someone with her particular skills. She resumed her seat to finish her cigarette and waited patiently for them to make their offer.

"We understand you are experienced in – should we say obtaining the confidence of persons of interest," the older one was saying.

Yolanda dragged her attention away from the faun to the older man. "So who would you wish seduced – and why?" she murmured.

"Seduce? What brings you to that conclusion?"

She laughed, a low, throaty chuckle that spoke of too many long nights of cigarettes and Pernod. "You people would never expect anything else." The cane chair creaked as she leaned forward to run her red nails across the older agent's knee. "Two questions. Who is my target and who is asking me to do this?" A fresh and uneasy quiet brought on another sharper laugh. "Come, gentlemen. Do you think me simple? I cannot be expected to risk my all without those basic facts."

The older man spread his hands wide and bowed in mock-courtly gesture. "You are right Madame. How very rude of us both. My name is Charles Fortier and my taciturn associate here is Jean Le Carreau."

Yolanda doubted either name was genuine but she smiled sweetly enough and returned his nod. "I am pleased to meet you, gentlemen. And you work for whom, exactly?"

Fortier flashed some form of identity card with a practised flourish that saw the wallet tucked back into his coat before she had read further than *Direction Generale...*

"We are civil servants, if you will, Madame Toureaux. Mere servants of the République. You need know nothing more," he said.

"And what does the République require of me?"

"We wish you to gather information vital for the safety of France."

Yolanda smoothed her skirt, hiding a bitter smirk. "You think a poor Italian widow is the best person to do this?"

"A citizen by marriage," Fortier replied. "And we were told you have the necessary ... credentials. You have some reputation for night life, though the ability to dance may not be enough for this job. I think this requires something additional that only a woman such as yourself can provide."

Yolanda glowered at them all in turn. She loved the bal musette with a passion, but she was well aware that many people frowned upon such places. Her husband's family for instance, something she had learned painfully when Jules died and her love of life was used as a weapon to deny her the basic rights of a widow. But that was the past. She was no prostitute. Yes, she fucked men in her work, but the money she was paid came for the information she gathered and not for the sex. It was a distinction she was careful to maintain and it made her angry that she needed to do so. When men like Fortier worked the same ploys, after all, they were not gigolos but dashing secret agents.

She felt the muscles in her jaw tighten and focussed on disguising a rising anger. The musettes were places where she gleaned the best information and made the best contacts. Fortier's insinuations that her intellect and usefulness was limited to her cunt was not even thinly veiled and was deeply insulting. She was no different to the thousands of young women who loved music and loved to dance, better than many because she was also a damned good detective; and she would prove that.

All eyes were on her, waiting for her reply through what had obviously seemed an extended pause. "It is necessary for my work," she replied carefully. "Monsieur Rouffignac here will tell you that I have collected a great deal of valuable information for his clients. And you have still to tell me what you wish to know."

"We have an assignment that could prove to be of great national import," said Fortier. "We wish you to befriend a man."

"Befriend? Is that all?" She waved her hand in dismissal. "Any woman could do that."

"This man is like no other man. Many have failed."

"Indeed?"

"Indeed. And those who failed are unlikely to know it because they are dead." Le Carreau leaned forward, fixing her from beneath his fringe with those odd eyes.

The flippant reply that had sprung to mind fled instantly. "How can it be that you ask me?" she whispered. "You don't have an agent in your department who is suitable?"

"We did," Fortier replied, "but…"

"She failed?" Yolanda said, her voice little more than a breath as the silence extended. "*They* failed? That does not inspire trust. You come to me because I am dispensable? The Italian widow without dependents?"

"That might be seen as a reason by some," Fortier agreed. "But not ours, Madame. You were recommended."

"By whom?"

"By someone who knows how your husband really died."

Yolanda looked away, studying the end of her cigarette. If these men knew something of Jules's death, the harsh facts – not his family's myth – and believed it gave her some kind of credential, then the wise thing to do would be to walk away. Though if they knew the truth, she had no choice but to stay, if only to learn the facts that had eluded her for so long.

"If it helps then you should know you have a vested interest of sorts in bringing these men to book," Fortier added. "Are you willing to assist us? If not for your late husband's memory then perhaps for a substantial consideration?"

There was no question about her wanting retribution for the death of her beloved Jules. Money only sweetened the pot. "How substantial?" She looked straight into the glacial eyes of Carreau. He knew, she was certain of it. He knew the truth.

"Ten thousand francs now and another fifteen, *should* you succeed," he said.

She nodded. Twenty-five thousand francs was more than she would earn in a lifetime at the factory. That alone should warn her of how high the mortality stakes were. She fought hard to still the tremors running through her. Since Jules had been taken by circumstances way beyond even her legendary control, his champagne life had little to offer. It was Jules that she missed, not his money. And Carreau did not believe she could succeed. Perhaps he did not know after all. "Twenty now and twenty more on completion," she growled.

"Done."

It was agreed so easily she wondered if she could have demanded more. "Details?" she snapped. "Where do I find this man? What am I required to coax from him?"

"His name is Etienne Plourde. He goes to several clubs but the most frequent stop of late is L'Arbre D'Argent."

Le Carreau slid a photograph along the desk toward her. A man of early to middle years stared out at her. He was of average height and build, dark haired and, Yolanda guessed, older than his baby features would suggest. The people around him were also from outside of the district. Two men and a woman, all in evening dress, which marked them as wealthy urbanites seeking thrills on the streets of Montmartre. She tapped a polished nail on the picture. "This club. It is L'Arbre D'Argent. I recognise the decor."

"Indeed. Our informants say we should expect him to be there again tonight, which is why the matter is of some urgency."

"And the woman? Who is she?"

"Thérèse Monet. Wife of Adrien Monet. He is the tall chap on Plourde's right. The older man is Karl Tildmann. We are told he is a mere clerk at the German Embassy, but his family were related to the late Kaiser. Tildmann is always armed and holds an implicit faith in the sanctity of diplomatic immunity. A privilege he has made free of on several occasions."

That made it easier. To have the wife of her target on the scene would have made things far more difficult. The wife of a friend she could deal with. She nodded and made to pocket the picture but Carreau was quicker, swiping it up and tapping it in a staccato beat on the edge of the table, and all the while staring at her with a pointed disinterest.

"What are Plourde and Monet supposed to be?" She gave Carreau a quizzical glance but aimed her words at Fortier.

"Plourde is a captain of industry." Fortier smoothed the hair at his temples. "You already work for Plourde, in manner of speaking. Wax polish and ammunition. I have no idea how the two businesses connect but it hardly matters. Monet has no profession. He is what the English would call a Gentleman. His family own considerable amounts of land both in France and Italy, and produce some very fine wines."

"And the connections between these people? Other than money."

"That, my dear, is what we would like you to ascertain. We have reason to believe they share quite strong political beliefs."

"Not communist, I would assume," she said.

"Far from it. We have reason to suspect Plourde is mixed up with La Cagoule."

Yolanda looked toward the ceiling to avoid the eyes of all three men. She did not like the way she was having to tease every tiny detail from these people. She liked the idea of infiltrating La Cagoule even less. Forty thousand francs was beginning to sound less enticing by the minute.

"I have no time for the demonising of political views. Spying on workers at the factory is enough, Georges." She looked her employer straight in the eye. "Working the factory floor gives me credibility and I tell you what I tell the owners there. It is not yet a crime to be either communist or fascist—"

"Unless it threatens the elected government," Carreau snapped. "You have French nationality through your marriage to an influential family, but be very careful. That can change, Madame."

Fortier held his hand toward Carreau, not quite touching him. "I am sure Madame Toureaux will be only to happy to help us, Jean. You should have more faith."

"Of course," he muttered.

There it was in a basket, and one of her own weaving. Had she not been so damnably arrogant, she realised, she might not have been delivered such a fait accompli. But once seen, these two could not be unseen. "So, you want me to seduce this Etienne Plourde? And then what?"

"If you succeed in coming to know Plourde then we shall move to the next stage." Fortier rose abruptly, bowing to Yolanda as he tugged his blue homburg on at a rakish angle. "Until we meet again Madame. I shall be in touch, Rouffignac."

~~~

Yolanda sipped at her second Pernod and continued her watch on the L'Arbre D'Argent. Plourde had yet to appear, and she might have been bored if her instincts were not telling her to be wary. She did not trust Fortier, and Carreau was plainly dangerous. But Fortier was paying good money for her to be here.

The herbal aroma of de l'herbe, could not quite hide

itself beneath the spicy Gauloises, and as the night drew on it was hard not to spot the junkers.

The dance floor at the L'Arbre D'Argent was small, barely room for twenty couples however intimately they shuffled in each other's arms through smoke that roiled on the beat of over-loud jazz. It created atmosphere, it was true, but she had never much liked L'Arbre. Its owner, Remy Billaud, was widely suspected of watering the wine, and his ten-year-old cognac was brewed weekly in the back yard, just a few feet from the midden which, she supposed, gave it the certain something – and it was largely to be avoided. She sighed gently in remembrance of the scents and flavours that she had grown used to with her well-connected husband, and wondered why the bright young things insisted on slumming it in Montmartre's cheap dives like L'Arbre. It certainly was not for the music.

She glanced toward the band and when the singer, teetering on the brink of the tiny stage, tipped her a mocking salute, she hid her smile, wondering if he realised what she was thinking. Had it shown in her face? And speaking of faces, she straightened in her seat to scan the crowd. Someone, lurking in the darkest recesses, had caught her attention. A face she knew. Not well, but seen recently, and in strange circumstances, of that she was certain. She had no time to track its passage through the melee; the doors opened on four newcomers, and the face was forgotten as Plourde and his entourage finally arrived.

Billaud hurried forward to evict a small group from their table for these honoured guests. He held out a chair for Madame Monet to sit whilst bowing further obsequiousness to her husband, and to Plourde and Tildmann in their turn.

Yolanda turned and nodded to her contact, Luc Marcel, seated at the far end of the bar. Marcel returned her signal and drained his glass in readiness, his lithe body sagging into the loose slouch of a man deep in the cups. She swivelled back to watch her target order a bottle of champagne. Marcel's information on Plourde's habits had been worth the money she had already been promised, and more. Her view of Plourde's table was perfect – as was Plourde's view of her.

On cue Marcel staggered away from the bar and stopped a pace away from Yolanda to chuck her under the chin, leering into her face. "Dance," he said. "You sit there like a queen all night and talk with no one. Dance with me."

"No. Go away."

Marcel moved closer, the edges of his rough-weave jacket rasping against her stockinged knee. "Too good for a place like this? We are too common for you? Is that it?" He made a grab for her and she delivered a resounding slap across a stubbled cheek and as he staggered back, a glitter of amusement flitted across his features at the strength of her blow. "Bitch!" he roared. "I—"

"Marcel. You are drunk. I've warned you before about this." Billaud grabbed him from behind and swung him toward the exit. "Go home to that poor wife of yours and be glad she hasn't yet slit your throat in your sleep." He gave the man a final shove and turned toward her. "Are you all right, Yolanda?"

"I am, thank you." She held a hand to her lips for a moment. "Thank you, Remy. I am so sorry, perhaps I should go."

"No. Stay for a while. Give him time to stagger home. If you want, I can get one of the boys to see you to le Métro?"

"That is good of you but I shall be all right."

A tiny smile tweaked at Billaud's dour features. "Let me know if you change your mind."

"I shall." She re-crossed her legs to allow her split skirt to fall open past her knee, and halfway to her hip, whilst gazing into the middle distance, being sure to give Plourde her best profile. When she was sure she had made an impact she adjusted her dress to a more demure display and unclipped her clutch bag for her silver cigarette case and went through the ritual of selecting a smoke, fitting it into the holder and reaching across the table for a book of matches.

On cue, an elegantly cuffed hand extended a Cartier lighter and flicked it into life. She lit up and exhaled a long plume before turning to look her gallant in the eye. She had seen the photographs but close up Etienne Plourde was a more startling man than she had expected, with deep-set brown eyes and hair that was not black as the picture had hinted, but a deep-auburn made darker by brilliantine. She caught a whiff of his cologne as he leaned in, all citrus and leather and money.

Yolanda turned slowly toward him and smiled. "Merci Monsieur."

"Will you join us?"

She gazed wistfully toward the doors and sighed. "I was waiting for a friend but he is so very late."

"Then he is a fool to leave a beautiful woman alone. Please—" Plourde gestured toward his table. "Join us,

Mademoiselle..."

"Toureaux," she said. "Yolanda Toureaux."

"Yolanda, such an exotic name. And your accent. You are Italian?"

"Yes."

"Ah. How charming. I can only apologise for my countrymen's boorish behaviour. A beautiful woman shouldn't be pestered that way."

"Wine makes a fool of the best," she replied. "Whatever their blood."

"You are too generous. Then may I at least offer you company? We can keep the wolves at bay until your friend arrives."

She paused for just a moment, maintaining the illusion of reluctance. "For a few minutes, thank you. If it is not an inconvenience, Monsieur..."

"Plourde. Etienne Plourde, and it is my pleasure, I assure you." He escorted her to the table and turned a chair from a nearby group for her to be seated.

"May I introduce my good friend Adrien Monet and his wife Thérèse."

Monet rose and held out a hand in greeting. "Enchanté." His grey eyes crinkled in good humour with a hint of a leer. Thérèse smiled tightly and inclined her ice blonde head with a pointed "Madame."

Yolanda grinned at her. Trust a woman to notice the wedding ring worn on her right hand, a sign of widowhood.

Plourde ignored Thérèse's ill humour. "And my close associate, Karl Tildmann."

"Mademoiselle." Tildmann took her hand and bowed sharply, wafting a small tidal wave of darkly spiced cologne.

Yolanda treated them all to an indiscriminate saccharine smile. She dismissed the Monets as exactly what they seemed. Thrill seeking, young and rich. Tildmann was different. She assessed him professionally as a danger to life. His hair was cut short but not shaved. Older than his companions by several years. Military and Prussian, judging by the small duelling scar along the edge of his cheek; and she could see why he was introduced as associate rather than mere friend because she very much doubted he had any. There was a shrewdness shared between him and Plourde that hand-stitched shoes and English suits only reinforced, yet there was an added hardness about the German that set him apart. Tildmann was something she had not seen before.

She took her seat between the men and treated them to extra smiles with added honey. "So, quite the greeting you all had from Remy. He is never so accommodating to the rest of us. Do you come often to l'Arbre?"

"Often enough to know you do not," Thérèse replied.

The smile Yolanda turned on the woman sparkled like iced diamonds. "I come here now and then. Not for a while it's true. I prefer L'Ermitage but my friend Jean asked to meet me here tonight." She shrugged her indifference. "But he's a bastard. I won't make that mistake again."

"He must be a madman to stand you up."

"Too kind." She sipped at the champagne Plourde proffered and looked around the club. "It is quiet in here," she added. "There must be something exciting happening elsewhere."

"There was a parade on the Left Bank today. Perhaps

they are all there?"

"I heard it was the Parti Communiste Français marching against les Camelot de Roi."

"Les Camelot are children," Monet growled. "They make noise and have no genuine cause."

His derision was palpable and she wondered if she had been given the wrong target. Monet was plainly the weak link amongst this quartet, but perhaps that in itself was the reason. Were she an agent of Cagoule, or more especially the more covert CSAR, the Comité Secret d'Action Révolutionnaire, she would not trust such a man with secrets of any value. "They are young, it is true, but that does not mean they lack passion. Far from it." Yolanda smiled at Plourde. "You seem amused, Monsieur."

"Passion," he said. "It should be kept for romance."

"You don't believe politics require passion?"

"Politics needs fire and great intelligence but always under complete control. Once passion enters the debating chamber reason leaves by the opposite door."

"You are a politician?"

"Not that you would recognise. I am but a humble cog in the wheels of commerce. But one dabbles."

"As one should." She grazed her fingertips along his sleeve to re-enforce her approval and noted his nostrils flare with an intake of breath. The bait had been taken. Now was the time to leave, to pique his curiosity. "Thank you for champagne, and I hate to drink and run but I must be going."

"Wait— Yolanda, will we see you here again?"

"Perhaps." She slipped her wrap around her shoulders, adjusted the scrap of veil on her hat and took another mental snapshot of the quartet. Monet and Plourde were captivated, and it had Thérèse Monet sulking and hostile. But Tildmann? His mood was altogether unreadable. The word that came to mind was "reptilian": cold and expressionless. She pulled her wrap close and switched her smile down to simper. "I may. Goodnight." She wove her way through the jungle of tables without looking back and stepped out into the night air.

The pavements were damp from a light shower and she cursed beneath her breath and held her hand out to test for droplets in the air. She glanced upwards at fast moving clouds scudding across the darkness alternately obscuring and revealing a moon that was already waxing past the first quarter. It could rain again soon, but it was not far to the nearest Métro stop.

Yolanda quickened her step, tip-tapping along a street brightened here and there by the open doors of clubs, spilling noise and light out into the dark. She rounded the corner and became aware of that same watchful feeling from earlier in the evening. She slowed for a moment, wondering if she should risk looking around and thus acknowledge her awareness, or walk a little faster. A bright neon sign gave her the opportunity to stop and read the menu attached to the railings marking a broad staircase leading to le Démon Rouge.

There was a shadow across the street. It had stopped as she stopped. It had the outline of something large, something with misshapen head and shrouded body. She felt a chill tweaking at her skin and rubbed it self-consciously away from her neck. The shape moved a little closer, coming to the very edge of the darkness, and she was certain she could discern eyes alive with inhuman fire despite the distance and lack of light. Nonsense, she knew, but the feeling of imminent danger was real enough in her imagination to contemplate descending into le Démon where there would be safety in numbers. She believed in trusting her instincts. Fortier's willingness to agree to such a high payment had made it very clear how dangerous this job was. Being followed by agents of le Cagoule, or worse, was proof enough.

An animal screamed, its shrillness tracing fingers of fear down her spine. *Perhaps some kind of cat,* she thought. Assuredly not human, and loud enough to pierce the raucous jazz exuded by the club. The shadow vanished. She did not see which direction it took, only that it was no longer there. Four seconds later a dog trotted along the far side of the street, head down, trailing some imaginary quarry, or perhaps that noisy cat.

Yolanda watched it slink away, quickening its pace as two couples left le Démon Rouge, chattering loudly in that way of the happy drinker, stumbling up the steps from the subterranean musette, necessitating her standing aside for them to pass. When she looked back the dog had gone, as was the shadow. "If," she muttered, "it had ever been there."

Yolanda drifted along in the wake of the chatterers, and was glad when they clattered down the steps into the Métro. At the top of the steps she looked carefully around her. The street was empty of pedestrians other than herself, and only a few cabs cruised along the avenue. No sign of shrouded figures or stray dogs. Not so much as a stray cat.

Whilst she waited for the train, with her back against

the wall, she scanned to right and left every few seconds, scrutinising each of the passengers strung along the platform. A group of noisy revellers were close by and there were several couples intent upon each other. When she boarded the train she eschewed her habitual luxury of a first class seat for the sake of company in second, yet watched her travel companions with deep suspicion. Couples holding hands or arms draped around each other, kissing, murmuring sweet things. Solitary travellers, several late workers intent on evening papers, a plumber with tool bag at his feet, two nuns sitting in tranquil silence. Yolanda was not religious but found their presence comforting. None of them exhibited the slightest hint of danger.

When she alighted at the stop close to rue Pierre Bayle her unease had dissipated, leaving her merely annoyed with herself for being so twitchy.

~~~

Visits to L'Arbre D'Argent fell into a pattern. Several times over the following two weeks she would arrive at L'Arbre, often to be welcomed into the group, and sometimes just the two single men, with Tildmann playing the part of exemplary chaperone. A charming if largely silent presence. He watched her like some battle-scarred Siamese cat. Pale of hair and skin, yet possessing points of dark intensity that were unsettling in the extreme.

The Monets, on the occasions they joined them, were full of gaiety and suspicion in equal quantities. Thérèse, in particular, left Yolanda in little doubt that her presence was not appreciated, though she suspected Madame Monet treated all attractive women with disdain; she was the kind to consider dominance over any masculine group to be hers alone.

Only Plourde's charm, and the money she earned purely in being there, kept Yolanda from slapping the woman's face raw and walking away.

Thérèse Monet aside, it was a curious courtship, far slower than Yolanda was accustomed to. In her experience, men of Plourde's kind did not wait for a relationship to evolve. She was almost surprised, then, to arrive late at the club and find none of the merry band at their customary table. It was almost midnight before Plourde hurried in.

"Yolanda, my dear." He crossed the room and bent to kiss her twice on each cheek and then lightly on her lips.

"Good evening, Etienne." Draping her arm around his neck she looked pointedly around her. "Did Karl get his meeting with the ambassador that he was talking about?"

"He did. There is a reception at his embassy tonight. I gather Herr Hitler himself will attend."

"And you are not with him?"

Plourde laughed. "Karl and I are friends, good friends, but not twins. Besides, I have no interest in Herr Hitler's doings — and the evening was nothing without you."

"Without me? How sweet." She picked up the glass of champagne that Plourde had poured the moment he entered the club and sipped, using the time to catch her thoughts. How had he known she would be there at all? Her visits seldom occurred on a Friday – that was one night she insisted was her own and not Rouff's to dictate. "And the Monets?" she said. "Are they joining us?"

"They remained at the embassy. Hers was a personal invitation, I gather. Thérèse's family are almost as well connected as her husband's."

"And our families are not? We shall have to be the proletariat. Vive la France. Vive la revolution."

His grin was lopsided, wry. "You were born Italian."

"I know. I was there at the time." She smiled at him from behind her glass giving him full benefit of her expressive eyes.

"Naturally, or you would not be here, and having you to myself tonight, that is to my great joy. But I meant that you would not understand how the rest of our little coterie feels about certain things."

"About revolution?"

He leaned forward, dropping his tone so that she strained to hear over the music. "Revival. Restoration."

"I thought your friends disapproved of les Camelot de Roi?"

"Only in terms of their methods. Le Cagoule have many of the same aims, and then there is CSAR."

Plourde's voice dropped away to little more than a whisper so that Yolanda lip-read the final word.

"CSAR? They exist? Are you telling me that—"

Plourde touched two fingers to her lips. "They do."

"All of them? But Tildmann is German, and surely such ambition would not sit well with the Reich?"

"Tildmann is his own man, and his involvement with the Party is—" He looked around them, pursing his lips. "We should not discuss such things here."

"Do you wish to go somewhere quieter?" She laid a hand on his arm and gazed at him from under her fringe. "Since we are alone."

He did not reply, only got to his feet and placed her wrap around her shoulders.

They took a cab to Plourde's apartment in the fashionable Sixteenth district. A grey stone building with ornate entrance. The obligatory concierge's hatch flicked back as they entered, and a pale jowly face watched them pass. Yolanda could feel dark eyes raking over her, taking in her clothes, her bearing, her demeanour.

"Bon chance, Madame Marchande," Plourde called, and Yolanda caught a disapproving snort as the hatch closed once more.

"She misses nothing," Plourde whispered. "Hard to entertain without her judgement, but—" He shrugged and pressed the lift button. "We have not had a theft in this building since she came here."

They rose to the penthouse floor and alighted in a spacious hall with a single door, and she realised that his apartment comprised the entire floor, a luxury that he plainly took for granted. Old money, she had little doubt, and it made her wonder yet again why he had chosen to bring her here when he could have been attending an embassy soiree, which the rest of the gang deemed so important. No doubt she would find out but she could be patient. This was the opportunity to gather the information that Fortier was paying for to drop right into her lap.

Plourde's housekeeper was still there despite the late hour and whilst he went to talk with her Yolanda prowled the salon with an expert eye. The room was not crammed with antiques, as she had anticipated it would be. The apartment might have been a film set, with a wide red Chesterfield sofa and deco volute swivel armchairs and glistening black side tables that were bare of ornament. She paused at the phonograph cabinet and lifted the lid.

A record perhaps? But no, it meant getting up to change it every few minutes.

She selected a music station on the wireless before drifting across to the short bookshelf. The books were generic, which she had not expected. Several classic novels. A few biographies. But what caught her eye was a hefty tome of myth and legend, lying on its side across the rest. Such an act of sheer slovenliness was so very out of place. She picked it out and opened it at random just as Plourde returned.

"You like to read?" He took the book from her and leafed through it, idly at first, and then with more urgency. His face gave little away but it was obvious to her that he was looking for something and had not found what he expected to find.

Plourde slotted the book casually back into the shelf, face down and spine in so that the title was obscured. "Not a good read," he said. "I was loaned it and haven't got round to returning it yet. Would you like a cocktail?"

"I would. A 75, if it's not too much trouble?"

"No indeed." He rang the bell and the housekeeper appeared within seconds, like a dumpy genii. "Mix a batch of 75s. And perhaps some olives?"

"Oui, Monsieur."

Plourde waved at the sofa and Yolanda lowered herself into it, running her hand over the plush red pile and smiling an invitation at him. "So, Etienne, here we are."

"Here we are," he agreed.

"We have never come back here from the club."

"No, there are places that I prefer to keep private."

"Even from friends?"

"Especially from *certain* friends. You of all people should know that. I did not realise until today that you were once married to Jules Toureaux."

He was watching her intently and she knew this was a test. Why he questioned who she was, Yolanda had no idea. Whether to dissemble or defend was a choice to be made in seconds.

"Yes." She laughed quietly. "Yolanda was his pet name for me when pillow talk was..." She paused and adjusted her face, knowing she had displayed her grief, but also knowing it gave her credibility, and hating that she had exploited a cherished memory so easily. "When he died, I kept it as a sort of keepsake. I have little else to remember him by. His family saw to that." She rose to stand in front of him, meeting his stare with wide and innocent eyes. "Does that worry you?"

"That you did not tell me your given name?"

"That I use the pet name given me by my dead husband."

Plourde pursed his lips, regarding her with bird-bright eyes, more hawk than dove. "Should it?" he murmured.

"Not to me. How did you know?"

"A little tidbit from Thérèse. I gather Adrien moved in the same circles."

"Ah." His emphasis on the whom made her flinch on the inside. She hoped it did not show beneath her smile. "Thérèse enjoys passing on such things. It makes her feel important."

"You noticed that in her."

"She is ... an excitable woman."

"Thérèse is an angry woman," he corrected her. "I'm not entirely sure why that is but she does seem to carry more ire than most. I gather Adrien was an old university friend of Jules. You know how that is."

He shrugged as if it explained it all. Yolanda hoped it was true, that her husband was the only part of her history that Thérèse had disinterred. "Poor woman. To store anger in such a way. It curdles the soul." She wrinkled her nose, her features crinkling into an impishness. "We Italians know how to release our anger into the breeze."

"Yolanda is not only an Italian name. It is also French. Did you know it means violet? It means to be strong?"

"As it does in Greek, also," she replied. "My mother had a passion for Greek myth."

"You also have passions. You are famous for it."

"Noi italiani?" She came to stand in front of him, tracing his lapel with her fingernail. "Or do you know something about me personally?"

"A little of both." He caught her fingers gently in his and raised them to his lips, kissing each of her fingertips in turn. "A passionate woman according to rumour and hearsay."

"Gossip seldom turns out to be true."

"Is that so?" His grip tightened, tugging her toward the corridor.

The master bedroom was as Spartan as the salon. No four-poster bed or brown wood chests and wardrobes, not even the latest in deco walnut wardrobes to relieve the monochrome decor. This was sleekness itself, and a complete change from her last sexual encounter – one of her choosing and not Rouff's. A quick roll amongst the trees of le Parc Floral, knowing the park keepers might stumble across them at any moment had raised its thrills, but the choice between damp grass and satin sheets was hardly a choice.

She kicked off her shoes and walked bare foot across the wide expanse of deep-piled white carpets. Two of the opposing white walls sported discreet cone-shaped lighting; on one they were set between vast windows and on the other poised between two deco canvases; Erte, she guessed. Doubtless originals. Yolanda could not imagine Plourde gracing his walls with mere prints. The third white wall housed two doors leading off, a dressing room, she imagined, and an en suite. The fourth wall was striped with wide vertical bands of quilted and buttoned white and black silk, which formed a vast headboard for the tennis court-sized bed covered in black silk.

Beside the bed was a table sporting a large cocktail shaker and a pair of paper-thin coupe glasses. It brought a wryness to her face. The housekeeper, like all good servants, had anticipated her master. It was slightly irritating to be so easily second guessed.

"Bathroom?" She walked toward one of the doors.

"Other one. You will find a robe in the cupboard."

The bathroom was yet another paean to ultra chic. There was a sunken bath as well as a shower cubicle that was almost as wide as her outstretched arms. She considered taking a long shower, such a luxury when the plumbing in her apartment was basic and frequently lacking hot water. But business before pleasure. She washed quickly and refreshed her lipstick and brushed out her hair before opening the cupboard.

The robe that Plourde had mentioned hung in the closet in solitary splendour; not the plain wrap she had imagined but a green silk chiffon peignoir and chemise, and in her size. Once again her presence had been both assumed and her seduction anticipated. In some ways it was flattering as it indicated at least part-mission accomplished. She had been angling toward this for weeks, so why did it give her the goose bumps? And not in a good way.

There was no doubt the robe was chosen to perfection. She hooked the peignoir closed and admired the way that it hugged her curves, twisting this way and that to catch herself from as many angles as possible in the fully mirrored wall. She turned finally to stare at her reflection, at how the green of her gown and red of her lips blazed against the monochrome setting. She stuck out, which was not a usual phenomenon. She was accustomed to standing out in a crowd when it suited her, and she certainly wanted Etienne Plourde to notice her for the next few hours.

The bedroom was empty when she returned. Drinks had been poured and she helped herself to one, sipping delicately, peering over the edge of the saucer-like glass as she toured with a more interrogatory eye. Without Plourde watching her could examine every niche, which took no time at all. Plourde's boudoir was impressive but depressingly sterile, with nothing of the man himself. The dressing room, however, showed some small signs of occupation. Suits and shirts hung in closets. Shoes stood in racks, drawers housed underwear and other items, yet not enough to indicate a long-term stay. All neat to the point of obsession. If she had to guess she would have said he had never lived here but used the place like a weekend retreat, or else he was more enigmatic than Robert Donat's Hannay.

Somebody, Plourde she assumed, was singing Bizet in a pleasing if muffled tenor. Maybe she had time to sneak back to the salon? Carmen's *Flowers* came to an abrupt stop and Plourde sauntered into the room, swathed in a midnight blue kimono. "Yolanda my dear." He pulled her gently down onto the bed and picked up the second glass. "To us."

Is this man being deliberately over the top? she thought, *or does he really think I'll be impressed?* She managed to mutter "to us" without laughing out loud.

Both drained their drinks and let the glasses fall.

Plourde was as flamboyant with his sex as she had feared, an arrogant lover, intent more on his own pleasure than hers, but sufficiently athletic to keep Yolanda busy. She could not fault his stamina, nor his reprise that came in short order. Finally, when he had fallen into deepest sleep around four a.m., with slow deep breaths just shy of a snore, Yolanda lifted a possessive arm from around her waist and slid from the bed.

The night, or rather morning, was warm but she tugged on the robe nevertheless. She herself was comfortable in her nudity but the notion that there could be someone else in the apartment, the housekeeper for example, made her feel vulnerable. There was enough light from the street to make it to the door without bumping or tripping, though there was little enough to risk collision. With a final glance back at Plourde's inert form she crept into the darker, windowless corridor.

Her first port of call was the salon. As in the boudoir, there was sufficient glow from streetlights through undrawn curtains to see the outlines of chairs and tables, and once her eyes were used to the dark she was able to tour the room with confidence. She was drawn to the bookshelf and the volume of folklore, but the space where Plourde had left it was vacant. The fact that Plourde had seen fit to move it gave the book a certain importance. She doubted its printed contents had much value, but maybe it had notes? Loose leaves or notations? She flicked through the other books, pages downward to dislodge any loose leaves, and found nothing.

"Where would he have put it," she whispered into the shadows. "There has to be a study, or another suite. Plourde has use of another bathroom?" She slipped back along the corridor, trying the next door, which proved to be the other bedroom. This one was smaller and less imposing, but somehow more human than the chamber of seduction. There was a bedside cabinet covered in the kind of thing one would expect from a room in use. A water carafe and a book. She picked it up, examining the dust jacket with a wry smile. "George Bernanos. That figures."

She set the book down and opened the draw of the nightstand and poked through the contents. Pens, a blank note pad with pages torn from the front, several packets of anonymous medicinal powders, and two neatly folded handkerchiefs. Nothing of interest. Nothing personal. Time and again that thought was coming to her. Nobody "lived" here – only visited now and then.

Turning to the bed she looked at the jacket that lay across the counterpane. She gauged it as hand tailored and for a far slimmer and taller figure than Plourde. An expensive item, fashionable and elegant, if unremarkable. Not Plourde's. His had no silk lapels and he never wore a patterned kerchief like the one folded neatly in the breast pocket. He favoured red or deep blue.

She laid it carefully back from where she had taken it and would have moved on had the ragged right cuff not caught her attention. Yolanda peered at it, going to the window and angling it toward the feeble light filtering from the outside to decipher the oddness of it. Something had made numerous attacks on the cuff, and whatever had been used was not sharp like a blade. She had seen the aftermath of enough knife fights to know that. Had the wearer been caught in a machine she had no doubt that the arm, or at very least the hand, would have been mangled beyond use. It seemed more that the sleeve had been snagged repeatedly by a blunt point, and then pulled free.

She rubbed the cloth between thumb and forefinger where it held a slight dampness and frowned at the ink-dark residue that clung to her skin. Lifting it to her nose she detected a hint of the butcher's block beneath a masculine cologne, dark and earthy. Blood and plenty of it – but enough to indicate the severe damage of a hand? Plourde had both of his intact as his use of them on her body had proved. She tweaked the handkerchief from its pocket and shook it out; felt the stickiness of some dark patches across its middle – and dropped it immediately.

A noise, a sharp rap came clearly to her, making the night feel all the darker and quieter. She froze, stilling her breath, tilting her head slightly to listen. A car swooshing along the street outside was faint but unmistakable, and the only sound for almost half a minute. Whatever she had heard inside the apartment was not repeated. Yolanda tiptoed to the doorway and stood inches from the opening, her breath held, but there was nothing to hear but the faint mechanical ticking of a clock somewhere in the apartment.

It had to be Plourde. Yolanda opened the door a little wider and scrutinised the passageway. Without windows every pool of darkness held a potential for menace. Each doorway seemed to shift as though opening slowly. That small table near the entrance loomed a deeper black than its surroundings. Had it been there when she arrived? For the life of her she could not remember.

She blinked in the hope that it would prove itself a mere shading. Lights from a passing car, even that fleeting light, showed that it too possessed an improbable shadow. She almost convinced herself that it was moving, pulsing like a black animal with four stiff spindly legs, and a strange hunching to its back; or was it a head thrown back toward her, with gleaming eyes watching from its middle? A glitter of teeth, pale against the night, revealed themselves and made her wish she had more to protect herself than a flimsy gown.

She glanced back into the room, wondering if it would be wiser to stuff the jacket through the window and climb after it rather than cross the corridor in that moment. Yes, she risked getting herself arrested even after the slim chance of survival from the drop of several floors – this against whatever that was in the corridor, in the dark, where she felt there was no chance whatsoever.

Gentle snoring from the main bedroom rose to a loud splutter. Plourde was shifting in his sleep, and slavering beast or not she could not risk him waking to find her prowling the premises. When she looked back at the beast it was gone.

Had it been there at all? she thought. *There's not even a table on that side, just an empty stretch of wall.*

Empty was all she needed to know as she scuttled back to the monochrome love nest where Plourde still slept. She stared down at him for a moment and then back to the door.

Plourde snuffled gently and turned onto his back, exposing an unblemished right arm where it lay across the space she had occupied a few minutes earlier. If she needed proof that the ruined evening suit had not been worn by him then this was it. She tiptoed to the bathroom and sat on the toilet, waiting for her bladder to cooperate, and peed with some force so that the noise of urine hitting water could not fail to reach the bedroom. She flushed the cistern, washing her hands with commendable vigour and padded back to her drowsy lover.

"I wondered where you had gone," Plourde muttered, as she slipped between the sheets.

His tone held an edge and she wondered if he had heard her enter the room. The ruined coat was real evidence of violence, and that was a distraction. And distraction was something she needed to employ on her own account. "Too much 75," she whispered. "But now I am refreshed." She slid a hand between his legs and tugged gently at his ball sack. "Are you?"

"But of course." Plourde's fingers fluttered across her left breast, and turned the move to a cupping – dropping his head to envelop her nipple between his lips.

Yolanda gave herself to the moment, since she was here. She enjoyed the sex, and it was a shame to waste a perfectly good erection.

Plourde was doing his own creeping about an hour or so later, just after dawn had begun to light the room with a faint rosy glow. She feigned sleep, listening as he used the bathroom and then crept around his dressing room. When the bedroom door closed behind him, she rolled onto her back and let out a long breath. White walls reflected the sunlight filling the room making it brighter than it had any right to be so early in the day. She narrowed her eyes against the sun's glare and sat up. It was time to leave.

She dressed quickly, wishing she had time to wash away the musky aroma of sweat and sex, in that gargantuan shower. But instinct was jabbing tiny needles in the nape of her neck, and ignoring that warning was never wise.

She wondered as she pulled on her stockings: *Why have I been so comprehensibly deserted at—* she glanced at the clock *—six in the morning?* She might have expected a farewell note from her lover. Its absence troubled her. Plourde had always played the gentleman with her and in his running away in the early dawn she might have expected at least a brief billet doux of the "call you later" variety.

The apartment was as quiet as a cathedral at dawn and about as welcoming to a sinner such as herself. She pattered across the salon to sweep for any sign of Plourde. Then on to the second bedroom suite, which likewise was empty. Even the blood-soaked jacket was gone. She passed through a series of rooms that she had not seen before and all were similarly devoid of anything she needed to see, and despite the housekeeper there did not appear to be any servants' quarters.

One final room remained unsearched: the dressing room of the second bedroom, which was securely locked.

Yolanda pressed her ear against the door, but could hear nothing. She bent and peered through the keyhole … and saw nothing. It was at times like this that she almost wished she was a heavier person so that she could attempt to kick in the door. Less violent techniques were more time consuming but she had become an accomplished lock-picker. A coat hanger from the bedroom supplied the means and she quickly fashioned the tools she needed. Applying tension to the bolt with one bent wire whilst lifting levers with a second. It was not a complex mechanism and surrendered easily to her touch.

The room was dark despite the sun streaming into every other room. Yolanda felt for a light switch and inhaled sharply at the display ranged around the tiny room. Weapons galore. Fire power enough to arm a small army, or a determined guerrilla group. She knew Plourde was a part of a dark and violent group. Several murders, executions in some eyes, had been attributed to them, but she had assumed from Plourde's manner that he preferred brains over brawn. Or perhaps even a walking wallet pay-rolling the secret society. But she would never have suspected him of role of quartermaster. Handguns, rifles, machine guns, and all the ammunition needed for a sizeable battle. So much that she wondered that the floor would take the weight.

She leaned forward to read the box labels. The German munitions, with their unmistakable swastika logo emblazoned across each package, were easiest to spot. There were also a few Italian items and some British. The remainder were French. Next to the munitions were banded stacks of leaflets. Some for les Camelot de Roi, others less specific in origin, calling for a return of the Monarchy. Not merely a right-wing sympathiser then, but an active co-ordinator. She took a sample of each leaflet, stuffing them into her brassiere for safety. They were as good as money in the bank, where her mission was concerned.

She looked around the room, sniffing in the scent of gun oil and cordite and something else she could not quite define – aromatic, heavy, spicy. At the end of the room was a large pair of cupboard doors. Something was considered worth stashing away from the rest of the goods. She wondered what Plourde found more valuable, more incendiary, than the items she had already found.

One way to find out. Taking a deep breath she flung them back and whistled quietly. An altar of sorts, which at first she assumed to be Catholic. Home altars were not uncommon. Her own mother's apartment had a niche for the Virgin and candles. There were the same goblets and candles here, but the symbolism— That was very different. No saints or virgins, only a squat statue of some dark creature of myth, with webbed hands and scaly back, and a tongue extruding from between fanged jaws. *Is it Greek? Egyptian? Sumerian, perhaps? No, this is something far less classical.* She picked it up to stare into its face and shuddered. *This is far older. This face is primeval, something that existed long before society recorded its fears on papyrus or paper, or maybe even in stone.*

Yolanda hesitated to name it as simply evil, if evil could be seen as such, but just touching it unsettled her. She set the creature down, turning it carefully to face the wall so that its fiery gaze and gurning leer could not seek her out like Odin's lance, before giving the rest of the altar her attention, noting the space at the centre where something had been removed – and recently by the way an outline had been left in the faintest layer of dust formed in days and not weeks. On the wall was an all-seeing eye in radiant gold and black above a circle of foreign glyphs. Not Masonic, because she had once been friendly with a Lodge official. Magical, she was certain. Black magic? Somehow she would have expected to see pentacles and inverted crosses for that. So what then?

After the statue the most prominent item was a long dagger resting on a black iron stand. A naked blade of the dullest black that may or may not have been metal. It felt cold under her hesitant touch, and was honed to a hair's width. The wood handle was a deeply polished, pitted with the small dents and patina that only extreme age could endow. Beside the dagger lay an old Luger service revolver, and next to that a small plain box. The blade she got: it belonged on an altar as would incense or candles. But a gun?

She lifted the lid of the box and stared at the handful of ammunition nestling in the old velvet interior. What made them unique was that each had been hand-cast in silver. She picked one at random and peered at it. Munitions of this kind were not an area of her expertise, though an old uncle back in Italy had kept a silver slug just like these "for the monsters". Yolanda had never asked what monsters and he had never offered to elaborate. Was this an affectation? A ritual item or some kind? Or was Plourde truly expecting to fight something supernatural?

He had left early and he had to know she would come across all of this. It bore all the signs of a setup, though she could not guess what he had in mind for her. Rouffignac had said Plourde had friends in high places, so arrest was the least she could expect, though she had a notion that any police attention she received, if caught, would be covered in a sheet for the court coroner's eyes alone.

She fumbled the shell with trembling fingers to join the folded leaflets between her breasts.

It was time to leave, though not, she decided, by the front entrance. The concierge, who had watched them enter, would notice that she left alone. Doubtless the woman would assume that Yolanda had been left suitable payment on the nightstand for her services. Or she may even be in the pay of this … cult – and set the hounds of hell on her trail. Yolanda laughed aloud as she exited the armoury. Her imagination, she felt, was running roughshod over logic.

She eyed the guns as she passed but left the weapons where they were. Her cleavage might hide a few sheets of paper and even a silver bullet but not one of these hefty Mausers.

Going to the rear of the apartment, she tried the door to the service stairwell. It was locked despite the fire-door bars. She made busy with her hangar wire once again and was soon pattering down to the street with shoes clutched in one hand, opening the street doors, and looking up and down the alley that ran along the back of the buildings. It seemed deserted though she knew that meant not a single thing, and choices had been taken from her. Hugging the wall of the apartment building to avoid being spotted from above she headed eastward, still barefoot to stop her heels making a noise in the quiet backway.

When she was a few metres from the main street she paused to tug on her shoes before walking briskly away from Plourde's building, her head down enough to hide her face from watchers, but her arms swinging free, looking for all like a slightly overdressed shopper with nothing more on her mind than the market that she knew would be found just two blocks away.

She had gone little more than a hundred metres, and was almost out of sight, when an explosion rocked the entire street. The blast propelled her forward and she felt the rush of the airwave showering her head and back with glass and chunks of masonry. She flung arms over her head and crouched low, out of instinct.

Debris had barely stopped falling before people were shouting and dogs were yammering at the outrage. A billow of dust and smoke still issued from the upper floor of the block she had just vacated. She felt her blood fizz with a cold thrill of knowing she had been inside just a few minutes before.

Though not yet eight o'clock there were a great many people on the street and most of them appeared to be pushing past her, which in itself drew attention to her lack of motion. A few people scuttled toward the impact although most were fleeing in the opposite direction, as only people who had known war, however many years past, could do. She joined the exodus and felt glad for a small tide of men and women, and one solitary dog, to camouflage her retreat.

She watched the hound pass and swore. Seeing the same dog twice was a coincidence, surely, but spotting this same scruffy street-mutt in as many days in as many districts was beyond suspicious. Yolanda glanced around to see if anyone seemed to be directing the animal but in such chaos it was impossible to tell. She was sure it had looked at her as it passed. It was out of sight now but that did not mean it could not see her. Nothing for it but to keep running and worry about the cur when she had time to catch breath.

The closest Métro stairwell was only a street away, but she wondered how safe travelling on it would be. If she was being watched, and she had no reason to believe not, then plainly she would be in danger waiting on a platform. Barring some bizarre coincidence, the explosion had to have been aimed at her, in which case Plourde or his associates would doubtless try again.

Or else it was aimed at Plourde, and that marked her as a potential witness to be tidied away at the first opportunity. Either way, she was a marked woman. Her work for Rouffignac had put her in the way of danger on several occasions but nothing quite like this, and it left her with one immediate course of action. She flagged down a cab and directed it to Agence Rouff.

~~~

"I am not sure that the money Fortier offered is enough."

Georges Rouffignac poured a generous tot of cognac into her coffee and handed her the cup. "Drink," he said. "For shock."

"It is not enough," she said again. "If I ever see it at all. I take it you haven't seen any of my cash as yet?"

"It never is sufficient, my dear girl. And don't worry, government departments never pay on time." Rouffignac's chair protested as he sat back, linking his fingers across his belly and regarding her from over his glasses. "You should know the address you went to was not Plourde's home." Rouffignac avoided her gaze by pouring himself a cognac despite the early hour. "His family own it, but officially the apartment has not been lived in for some months."

"That does not surprise me. It felt sterile. Nothing personal there. Like a very expensive hotel room."

"Essentially it was. Now – this blooded coat. You say it was Tildmann's? How can you be certain of that?"

"I am as certain as I can be. It wasn't Plourde's. The wearer had to have considerable injuries and Plourde had none. And if I was to hazard an educated guess, I would say Tildmann. If that was not his dress jacket then it was one uncommonly like it. I have seen him wear it a dozen times."

"One evening jacket is very like another. Why are you so sure?"

She shrugged. "The German tailor's mark."

"Fair enough. So was Tildmann there?"

"I never heard a thing. But it is—" She pursed her lips, looking down at her hands clasping and unclasping. "It *was* a substantial apartment. When Plourde was not in the boudoir as I came out of the bathroom I assumed he had just gone to shower in the second suite. But he could as easily have gone to talk with someone else."

"And if that is so, then they doubtless saw you searching."

"I did think I saw something." She shuddered, remembering the creature in Plourde's hallway. It was tempting to tell Rouffignac all about it, but it sounded insane to her own ears. She wasn't about to have him think her crazy. "There were no lights burning so anyone could have been hiding," she said. "My imagination ran a little wild."

"I shall pass these leaflets onto Fortier. But this—" he tapped the silver bullet "—you say there were a lot of these?"

"A box full."

"What do you think they are for?"

She shrugged. "I have the impression Plourde is afraid of the unknown, of things beyond sane reason. The armoury was also an altar, but to what or whom?" She shrugged, her hands held palm upwards. "Nothing I have ever seen before. Nothing this side of insanity."

"Sanity is overrated. Reason is another matter." He opened the draw of his desk and swept the piece of silver into it. "I have seen many things done for a variety of reasons that are far from sane. I would not be too quick to question Plourde's mind."

"He believes in what? Ghouls and ghosts?"

"I think he is more concerned with protecting himself."

"Which has not been very successful."

"You are assuming he was the target of the assassination?"

Hearing her boss voice fears she had already raised with herself rattled cold chills down her spine. "It may have been an accident."

"And the sky is green." He tossed a folder onto the desk in front of her. "According to sources, Plourde was at the embassy party. He was seen to arrive early with the Monets and left shortly after dawn. A dead body in his apartment, when he was seen elsewhere by half the diplomatic community of Paris? This explosion will be reported as a robbery gone wrong. Or else revenge by a woman he had been seen with but was excluded from a prestigious event."

"Nice. Except there will be no body."

"Indeed."

"So what now?"

"I shall call Fortier and ask him about the money. Meanwhile, go home and get some sleep. And be careful."

"Should we call the Sûreté? Do I need protection?"

"You may well need protection from the police if you admit you were in that apartment this morning. Think about it my dear. Don't you feel it a little odd that you had just left when the bomb went off? Had they wanted you dead already then…" He shrugged at her sour expression. "I suspect the arms and ammunition were the target. It was quite possibly not even Plourde or Tildmann who detonated it."

"Who then? Fortier?"

He shrugged. "You are alive. Be glad, my sweet girl."

"Easy to say when it is not your hide. Can't you call your friend, Commissioner Badin?"

"I will but it will take time, and I suspect he would still be forced to arrest us both. An attack on that part of town will have the city fathers baying for blood, and Plourde's fascist thugs have some influential friends."

She nodded. As Laetitia, wife to a man of breeding, she had seen first hand how the upper echelons closed ranks in times of need. People could and had vanished for far less than causing an explosion in a well-heeled part of town. "So we are on our own?"

"We have Fortier's department."

She frowned at him. "Given that he may have lit the fuse, I am not reassured."

"We have no evidence of that. But if I am honest,

neither am I reassured."

"But the money is good." Yolanda finished her coffee and got to her feet. "I shall await your call Georges. Au revoir."

~~~

The three days that followed were a haze of disturbed sleep. Laetitia had not been prey to irrational fears in all the years she had done this work as Yolanda. Rouffignac's insistence that she had been allowed to escape Plourde's apartment alive was small comfort. As plain Laetitia she was convinced that she was being followed at every turn – and was certain she had spotted that wretched cur at least twice.

When her brother Riton called and demanded she come dancing or be declared a square she finally gave in, grateful to return to her beloved bal musette without fawning over Plourde and his cronies. She hoped Fortier would see her work as done and pay her the money as agreed, but as the days wore on she became increasingly anxious on that score. And now Rouffignac was not returning her calls – either as Yolanda or Laetitia.

She sat at her dressing table carefully applying make up and trying hard not to allow instinct to dictate her life. On the one hand, the impulse to lock her door, pull the bed covers over her head, and wait for it all to go away was overwhelming. On the other, fleeing the country had a nice ring to it. Either way, she needed money and that was in short supply until or unless Fortier and Carreau came up with the goods. And the more days that passed in isolation, and without any hint of the promised recompense, the more she feared that was not about to happen. Another night stuck in her apartment all alone, listening for every creak on the stair, was going to send her over the top.

A final fluffing of powder and she sat back to give full scrutiny to the results. The bags beneath her eyes told their own story but she had them disguised pretty well. The dress she wore was new. An elegant figure-hugging pleated suit in green silk that was a birthday gift, hand stitched by her mother. Doubtless a copy straight off the catwalk because her mother was gifted in cutting patterns from a single sighting. Laetitia did not need anyone else to tell her that it made her look good. She pinned a neat white pill-box hat onto her platinum blonde bombshell coiffure and turned her head this was and that to admire the effect. She had hoped the new hair would deflect any recognition on the street but knew it would fool nobody who knew her well. She was both Laetitia and Yolanda and would remain so all the time she was here in Paris.

One final spray from her atomiser and she was ready. Laetitia trotted down to the front hall, waving to Madame Pennet lurking somewhere in the depths of her concierge kiosk, and emerged into the daylight.

Rue Pierre Bayle was bustling with residents out to enjoy the holiday treats of a Pentecost Sunday already thick with heat. Watching the street for a few moments, looking for the untoward and seeing nothing out of the ordinary, she started down the street toward le Métro station, Phillipe Auguste.

Halfway to the junction she spotted the dog lying in the shelter of a small car, his eyes half closed, and panting in midday warmth. His head swung toward her and his eyes were wide open now, meeting her gaze without any pretence of coincidental meeting. She looked around for a sign of man, or woman controlling this hell hound. As before there was nobody. Laetitia lowered her head to return the mutt's glower. It was as Yolanda that she looked away, glancing left and right, searching again for who might be even vaguely connected with him.

The dog heaved himself to his feet, shaking out ragged curls, and took a few steps toward her. His head was low, his eyes still fixed on hers. There was no mistaking the menace in his pose. There was no mistaking the odd eyes – the evil eye of the fairy realm, some would say. There was only one person who would have a dog with such an aberration, yet there was no sign of Carreau anywhere. She looked back at those eyes.

"Carreau," she muttered. "I may be insane, but somehow…"

The dog's lips pulled back to display yellowed teeth.

"Ooh, is it the name? Hey Fido?" The dog had reacted to the word "Carreau", that much was obvious. She was not sure she wanted to acknowledge her immediate suspicion that she was somehow faced with a creature imbued with the persona of a human.

Yolanda waited for a gaggle of young women, straggled five abreast across the paving, to reach her position. As they drew level with her she slipped behind them and scuttled in the opposite direction from the dog, stepping out as fast as she was able to the end of Pierre Bayle without running, and turned left.

She glanced back and saw the canine sitting at the junction, watching her intently. The street traced the cemetery wall and bent at Chemin de Ancient Ports. The way ahead was blocked by a pair of lorries nose to nose across the road. A casual observer might think it was accident from the shouting and gesticulating between drivers. Yet she could see no damage to either vehicle, and the arguments were rather half-hearted, artificial.

She contemplated a sprint past them until one driver took a length of pipe from the back of his lorry and turned to face her. She was being herded through the cemetery gate. *But that,* she thought, *may not be so bad. There at least I might have some advantage.* Le Cimetière du Père-Lachaise was familiar territory and there was an outside chance her pursuers were less acquainted with its many paths than herself. Of course, most of Paris had a loved one somewhere along tree-lined streets of serried tombs and memorials, but she had to take the chance.

The cut of her suit was hampering her somewhat but she managed a fair turn of speed, tip-tapping past the graves at not-quite a trot. Being Pentecost Sunday, the graveyard was awash with families carrying flowers to honour the dead, which she took as a good thing. In theory, an attack was far less likely in a crowded place, except that she had reached a quiet junction where three paths met around a large grey edifice that bore no family name. She was wondering which way to go when the hound reappeared on the path ahead. Yolanda veered toward the next junction. Once again the dog was there, sitting in the very centre of a path. Not doing anything, just sitting, blocking her way.

"Shoo," she hissed. "Go away." Her heart was pounding, partly from the speed of her walk but also from fear. The dog stared at her, head on one side, panting loudly.

"Shoo!" She bent to pick a stone from the side of the path and shied it in his direction, striking him square in the head. The dog let out a yelp and back pedalled, but did not flee.

Why was she being foolish? It was just a dog, however well trained, that had yet to come close enough to pose a genuine threat. *And if Carreau wants to do me harm there are far more effective methods.* Walking slowly, with head up, avoiding eye contact yet aware of every hair on the dog's neck that ruffled in the breeze, she moved forward.

The mutt rose, paws planted firmly apart, and uttered a low growl.

She took a few more steps, still watching her adversary from the corner of her eye. The growl became a snarl, the grizzled nose wrinkling, his lips pulling back to reveal glistening canines. He placed on paw in front, a deliberate act, full of challenge, and the growl became a whine.

She backed up and stopped again as a grating voice bad her to "wait".

The hound surged forward, pushing past her toward the huge mausoleum surrounded by railings that stood at the centre of the crossing point.

Yolanda spun around, eager to keep the new creature in line of vision. It – he – was almost two metres tall, with wide shoulders and narrow hips. It wore a bulky jacket despite the sultry weather, with hood up, putting much of the head into cover.

She had an image of a broad skull that seemed wider even than its heavy brow should make it. Twin rows of jagged teeth in a toad-wide lipless mouth were barred at the dog standing between him and his prey. Yolanda had no doubt that firstly this thing was not human, and secondly, she was the object of his attention.

Against her better judgement she met the creature's

gaze for a briefest instant and her world took a sideways step, leaving her senses far behind her. It took all of her concentration to remain upright. She would have run, had her legs been able, but the voices in her head were telling her to sleep…

The dog ululated in a manner no common hound had a right to do. The beast snarled a rabid retort, the noise catching in his throat as he breathed raggedly, slavering spittle and bile.

Without warning they flew at each other in a flurry of noise and limbs, rolling over and over until they hit a kerb and separated. The beast took flight with hound in noisy pursuit and both creatures scrabbled over the railings and into the shrubbage surrounding the mausoleum.

She was alone in a quiet moment – a faux peace broken by bird song and then the distant voices of families wandering the graveyard paths. And the pounding of her heart rattling beneath her ribs. Her conscious thoughts wavered like a winter deluge running down a windowpane. As the miasma gradually cleared, she looked all round. Not a living breathing thing in sight. Not dog nor monstrous man, nor whomever had spoken to her, as she had very nearly lost reality. She had to make the logical assumption it had come from somewhere within the maze of grave markers and tombs. The mysterious controller of her mystery canine.

Her legs had ceased their trembling and she felt her mind becoming her own again and she knew that waiting in this desolate corner would be a poor choice. She knew where she was and knew she needed to be elsewhere. Instinct drove her toward the nearest point of refuge.

Hurrying down the righthand path and left at the next

junction she was soon standing in a row of larger family mausoleums. Square blocks with classic columns and porticos over metal-clad doors, many secured with substantial padlocks. Most were enclosed within railing fences giving the appearance of some macabre suburbia of death. Yolanda counted along the row out of habit and stopped at one of the Romanesque frontages. The plaque over the doors was carved with a single word. TOUREAUX.

It was Laetitia who unlatched the gate set in the iron railed fence and rested a hand on the studded oak door. She had no key to enter and this was the closest she ever got to her husband's final resting place – his family had seen to that – but she derived comfort from even this proximity, along with an abiding sadness. She seldom came here, despite living so close. She didn't think Jules would mind, considering how he died, which made her smile, wondering what he would have made of her new blonde hair. He would have laughed, she was fairly certain. He would have run his slender fingers through it and pulled her close and buried his face amid the waves, sinking beneath their shiny surface to nibble at her ears, her neck, her throat. It was Laetitia and not the nebulous Yolanda who let out a small moan, tensing her muscles around the memory of his cock...

The clock on the nearby tower chiming the half hour broke her remembrance. A shudder ran through every part of her that she turned it to a shake, chiding herself for such a sinful waking dream in this of all places. The clock also reminded her that she was supposed to meet Riton in twenty minutes. Laetitia leaned forward, her lips against the crack between the double doors. "Goodbye, Jules," she whispered. "Until we meet again."

"Let's hope that won't be for a while yet."

The voice was one Laetitia/Yolanda did not know well, but still recognised with a sinking in her gut.

"Carreau." Yolanda walked back to the path to face the agent, noting how they were the same height. "Whilst I appreciate your sentiment this is neither the time nor the place." She ran her hand through her hair, aware that it was unruly from her scamper through the cemetery. "How can – oh, you're bleeding."

"Am I?" he dabbed the cut on his hairline and then examined the crusted residue adhering to his fingertips. "You're a good shot."

"Me?" She quirked her eyebrows. "Why would I do such a thing?"

"Because you are good at whatever you do." Carreau looked back along the path, head raised, his nostrils flaring.

As if scenting the wind, thought Yolanda. *Not the handler then, but a lone wolf.*

"Come. I hate to hurry you away from your dead, on this day of all days, but we need to leave this place." His fingers curled around her biceps, squeezing the muscle painfully, and steered her toward the exit. And since she was going in that direction Yolanda allowed herself to be guided through the main gates.

They took a short and silent walk to a small cafe that still gave them some view of the gates. Carreau chose a table from where he commanded a good view of the street, and she noted how the seat he assigned himself was backed against the wall – just as she would have done. Yolanda asserted control of herself once more and was eager to show this man how she was not intimidated.

"Coffee?" He gave no time for her to reply, signalling the waiter with a snap of his fingers. He spooned five heaps of sugar into his cup and stirred carefully in an uneasy silence. "You should not be in the city," he murmured at last.

"I would be gone already but how can I when I have no money? Fortier promised so much and I have not seen one solitary sou."

"Money will not help if that creature had caught you." He was watching the bubbles racing each other round the top of his cup and when he finally looked up Yolanda felt his odd coloured eyes like twin spears slicing at her, ripping Yolanda away and leaving Laetitia exposed and shivering.

"You coloured your hair," he said.

His abrupt change of subject confounded her further. "I thought it might help. New look. New—"

"How do you think it would help? Same address, same habits. You even visit your husband's grave. A bottle of peroxide is hardly going to help against the likes of Tildmann. He has the scent of your blood and bone. You could paint yourself green and call yourself a cabbage and he would still know you."

It made no sense but it made perfect logic, and good to have her suspicions validated. "So that *thing* was Tildmann?"

Carreau shrugged. "Yes. Or one of his type."

"And you? What are you, Monsieur Carreau?"

His lips curled, displaying long canines that she felt sure had not been so pronounced when they had first met. "I am of a 'kind' but one of a different kind. Though sometimes…" He shrugged. "I owe you a debt. For Jules."

"You knew him? More debt? On top of my forty thousand francs?"

"A tale for another time," Carreau replied. "If we survive this day I shall tell you all. Our priority is to get you away from here. Fortier does not care that you are being hunted. He has the information he needed, and Plourde's arrest is certain if he is ever found."

"Did Plourde plant the bomb, or was that Tildmann? Or even you—"

"Not us. Fortier had no further use for you but he has need of Agence Rouff." His shoulder lifted in a small gesture of resignation. "It was not Fortier. It was one of Tildmann's agency. You should have been killed but you are a lucky woman. The timer was faultily set."

The image of a creature in Plourde's hallway flashed into memory. "I saw it. I think." Her face clouded. "Like that thing back there. I don't understand any of this. I mean, what are they? I get the wearing masks to disguise themselves but if I can't recognise them why pursue me? Are they sent by the Reich?"

"Fire is a speciality of Tildmann's kind. And no, not from the Reich, as such, though the creatures were summoned here by the meddling in things the officers of the Reichstag do not comprehend." He growled the last, a deep vibration deep in his belly that reminded her of the dogs her grandfather had kept on the farm back home in Italy. She started back, the fear she had felt in the cemetery returning in a rush.

Carreau stretched across to envelop her wrist in one vast hand. "Do you want to know more? I can tell you. It may help you survive. But you must remain calm."

"I want to understand," she replied.

"Then know this. Most governments have a vested interest in supernatural elements. Not just Herr Hitler."

Yolanda laughed, sharply but with an edge of brittle fear. "Oh really—"

He tightened his grip on her wrist. "All of them. Trust me on that. Religion lends them the means. A cover, if you will. It is just that the Reich pursues that interest more openly than most. They came across Tildmann and believe he is their ally. They think they have the means to control him. They have been led to believe that until now, but his kind won't be contained for long."

"You keep saying that. His 'kind'."

"Demons." The word came low and casual and he watched her intently, those odd-coloured eyes unblinking in a darkening face. "You don't believe me. I see it in your face. Tell me, do you believe in gods?"

"I believe *in* God," she snapped.

"Gods," he replied. "Plural. Demons go with the territory. Your own countryman Dante wrote about it. *The Inferno* has many inconsistencies, but one thing it has right is the existence of demons."

His logic was irrefutable and totally unacceptable. All of her life she had knelt in the cathedral stalls muttering novenas for saints and supplications to the Madonna and Child. A lifetime habit. She had never questioned it, or considered the implications of the fallen. "Demon," she repeated.

"Believe it. And you have come to the attention of the Horde. They have your scent, and they will not permit you to escape a second time. If you wish to survive we shall need a very careful plan of action."

"I have no idea what you seek to gain with this nonsense. The only thing I need is my money and I would leave right now. Go to America maybe." She wrenched her hand away and glared at him, pointedly rubbing at her wrist. "Get me my money and you will never see me again."

For a moment she thought he was going to strike her, public place or not, and lifted her chin defiantly.

"These are not hoodlums you can charm into submission," he said. "The only way you will hope to deal with them is to kill them. Which is easier than you might think. This one that calls himself Tildmann is a minor creature. He has power but he is not so invincible as he likes to pretend, or you would be dead already. Avoid looking him in the eye. He has the power of Mesmer."

That she could believe, remembering how she had been close to passing out in the cemetery.

"Can you shoot?" Carreau demanded.

"I can."

He reached inside his jacket and, glancing quickly around him, took a weapon from an inside pocket, wrapped a serviette around it and slid it across the table, its faint metallic scraping setting Yolanda's teeth on edge. "It's a MAB model C. It fires just six rounds so don't use it unless you are pretty sure you're going to hit whatever you aim at. It's accurate enough at close quarters but if you have to use it on that creature keep firing until it stops moving. One slug will not be enough. Even the ones I've loaded in this clip will need time to take out a demon."

"Are they silver?" She thought back to the ammunition she had seen in Plourde's apartment.

"No, but they contain elements that are toxic to his

kind. And not all that good for yours, as it happens, so don't handle the clip any more than you can help. I will have your money tonight." Carreau gestured at her outfit. "You were going somewhere?'

"To L'Ermitage. I thought a public place would be safer."

"Good thinking. Do not on any account go home. Stay in your public places for the rest of the afternoon and then you must catch the 18:25 Métro from Porte de Charenton. Is that clear?"

"And you will have my payment? All of it?"

A curt nod told her everything she wanted to hear. She smothered his hand with her own slim fingers and smuggled the MAB pistol into her purse. "18:25 at Porte de Charenton. I shall be there, Carreau. Make sure that you are."

The bell above the cafe door clattered like a mocking applause for her exit as she stepped out briskly, aware of gooseflesh pimpling her arms despite the sun. Carreau was obviously mad. There was nothing to explain the things she had seen other than masks and subterfuge, and there was no reason to believe the agent would keep his word, yet what choice was there?

Laetitia was gone and Yolanda had returned, taking the next turn, heading for the bus stop that would take her to meet her brother and his friends. She walked quickly, eager to get away from the cafe, the cemetery, and Carreau's madness, and eager to get to L'Ermitage before the dark clouds gathering over the city chose to perform.

She failed to notice the dog until she was about to leap onto the bus platform. A sharp pain in her left hand made her wince but it was only when she took a seat and searched for her fare that she noticed the blood. Not a torrent, just an oozing from a small nick to the side of her hand. Yolanda sucked back the iron taint and looked back through the rear window of the bus. *What in hell is that creature doing?* The bite was not bad, more a graze. She had done worse operating the machines at the factory. What hurt her was that it had happened at all.

Being the Sunday of Pentecost, with all of the holiday atmosphere it brought about, the bus was packed with families. She smiled at a pair of small children with their parents, obviously up from the country, dressed in their best, carrying flowers with small bells attached to ward off evil spirits. *Apposite, in a macabre fashion,* she thought. She looked back at the way she had come, but though she could see the bus stop the hound was out of sight. Maybe the bells had worked.

She sucked again at the bite and fished for her handkerchief. If she got blood on her new suit she would shoot that dog with his own damned gun.

~~~

L'Ermitage was busier than usual, full of holiday joy with dance and song, though many were out in the gardens trying to avoid the oppressive humidity. She sat with Riton, watching their friends Pierrette and Maurice dance a valse musette with more vigour than style, and calling to the accordionist Jean Salimbeni to "play faster".

"So, you will be leaving us today," Riton said.

"I must."

"What should I tell Mother?"

"That I have gone on a vacation."

"She will be heart-broken."

"I will come back when it is safe." She was beginning to wonder why she had told her brother she was leaving. His questions about the explosion that had come close to killing her, and his constant references to her visits to L'Arbre, had her concerned. She thought she had told him enough to silence him. Perhaps it would be enough to keep him from asking questions elsewhere, from attracting attention of Le Cagoule, or worse.

She leaned her left elbow on the table's edge and rubbed at her temple with stiff fingers, breathing in cologne sprinkled on the handkerchief neatly tied around the dog bite. Her head ached abominably and her hand itched like a dozen tiny bee stings. She was aware that her fingertips were losing sensation so that it might have been the hand of a stranger easing the throb in her skull. It was hot and the odour of unwashed bodies added to the stale beer and cigarettes.

Yolanda breathed in the floral scent and envied Maurice and Pierette out on the dance floor. Almost anywhere would be preferable to this tortured conversation. "Tell no one, even Mother, for as long as you can. I only tell you so that you can protect yourself. Plourde saw you several times with me. He might try to force my whereabouts from you."

"But you won't tell me," Riton snapped. "What about my lessons?"

"I have paid Jean for those. And as for where I am going?" She tapped the side of her nose. "If I don't tell you then you can tell whoever asks that your bitch of a sister would not tell you anything. Only that she was going for a holiday." She felt their conversation had boarded a carousel, forever turning and dipping and going nowhere for all of that. Riton was not the brightest. She loved him dearly but he really was quite stupid at times, and selfish because it was not their mother he cared about right now, but his lifestyle that came from her purse. She looked at her watch. "I must go soon."

"To start your wonderful vacation? Bon voyage."

"You are going away?" Pierrette flopped down next to them and took a mouthful of coffee, grimacing at its temperature. "You never said. We've hardly seen you for weeks and you want to leave us already."

"I'm sorry. I have neglected you all terribly— Come with me now, Pierrette. I have an appointment to keep, but after that we can have a wonderful evening. A celebration."

"But it's thundering out there now – it will rain soon." The younger woman pouted prettily. "My hair will get ruined. Go, do whatever you must, and meet us here later."

A shimmer ran through Yolanda as she thought about the liaison ahead of her. She felt unwell. Perhaps more rattled by the dog bite than she had realised. Her head swam every time she turned too fast, and her limbs ached abominably. She was not given to nerves yet the thought of going alone to meet Carreau had her sweating. "Please. For me?" she pleaded.

"No. I promised Jean I would sing for him in his next set. But here—" Pierette reached down beside her seat and retrieved a small parasol "—take this. You can bring it back later."

Yolanda had an idea Pierette's excuse was made to punish her for neglect but the gesture of the parasol touched her. Uncharacteristic tears were simmering behind her eyeballs. "I'm sorry." She looked at her watch. "I must go."

"But we shall see you later? You promise?" Riton's tone, with its mix of hope and resignation, twisted the knife. She had no intention of hurting those close to her; it was an unfortunate byplay to her chosen course and she so regretted that sad-horse look on his features.

"But of course. An hour. Two at most." She flicked his arm with her gloves and grinned. "Will you still be right here?"

There was a flicker of concern in his face but he said nothing, only nodded and told her to, "Go then. Look after yourself."

Yolanda distributed kisses and wafted away from them as elegantly as she knew how. The heavy door closed with the familiar basso boom which had earned it the name of le Tambour. It was so familiar to her yet knowing today might be the last time it beat its note for her, it felt so alien. So final. She flipped the parasol open and shook her head at its lace awning; exquisite, but little defence against the weather. Large spots were beginning to fall as she stepped onto the bus. Thunder rattled at the windows and reminded her of a newsreel she had seen of a vast temple bell being struck with a pole.

The conductor was a regular on the route, whom she knew by sight.

"Just in time," she shook out the parasol and laughed, handing over the exact fare. All should be normal in his world.

"As always. Going home already?"

"Not yet. I have a meeting." She winked at him and made her way to a seat, letting him make of that what he would.

At the Porte de Charenton she had to run through the rain and push through the crowds of Pentecost picnickers eager to hide from the storm, buying tickets to anywhere with a roof to shelter beneath. Having a book of pre-paid tickets, she had no need to queue and made her way down to the platform, which was no less crowded than the ticket hall.

As the Métro tender rattled alongside the platform the crowd surged forward as one to the second-class carriages – as was to be expected in such a district.

Yolanda stepped into the first-class carriage and selected one of the leather seats. There were plenty to choose from – it was completely empty. She stood up again, angry and ready to leave. *Where is Carreau? The Bastard. He's let me down.*

A blur in the corner of the compartment made her pause, and the doors had closed before she identified the movement as a large dog crawling from beneath a bench. The train moved away with a jolt that tipped her back into her seat.

She dared not move her attention from the dog. All around her had fallen silent and still. No rumble of engines and wheels, no rush of air, no vibrations or swaying.

The dog stood staring at her, and then he rose up on his hind legs, stretching out taller and wider, limbs paling to white hairlessness, his head re-assembling before her eyes. The muzzle shrank back, the forehead widened. Those teeth dissolved behind lips. Real lips, sensual lips smiling at her. A man. A *naked* man. Carreau.

She looked him up and down with amusement tinged

with appreciation. His were whipcord muscles rather than bulging biceps, but the power in them could not be argued. They held a latent energy of hard-won stamina. Thin lines of old scarring criss-crossed his skin, some ancient, some less so, and so many that not a single hand span was free from them.

Except perhaps his groin. But then what man would not protect that the most? The thought amused her so that she struggled to keep the smile from her mouth.

The object under inspection, and she did not doubt that he was now human in any accepted sense, stepped behind a seat to hide his body from waist down, and reached up to a luggage rack to pull down a bag.

"Yours," he said.

"Is the dog gone?" She knew the answer but had a perverse need to hear him admit the truth.

"The dog – is right here. Look, I know it is hard to accept, and most people forget as soon as they walk away. It is how they deal with it. But I am—"

"Loup Garou." Admitting this fact out loud was a relief to her. Part of her, the sane part, she assumed, had not wanted to acknowledge it, but she had seen enough in the past week to entertain just about anything, including the living breathing myth dematerialising before her eyes. "I heard tell you were all about night-time and moonlight."

"There are a lot of untruths told about me."

"Well, here is one truth. You bit me."

Carreau shrugged. "It was necessary."

"It was—" The man was insane, or else she was. Yolanda blinked hard. A trickle of sweat ran between her breasts, and a sheen of perspiration forming on her face as if influenza had taken hold of her. Carreau's face swam back into focus. "It was evil. Just give me my money and we'll forget we ever met."

"Not before we finish the plan."

He was mad, she was certain now. But she could not summon the energy to rail against his insanity. "We have a plan now? You never mentioned a plan."

"I've always had a plan, but this one happens to have changed since this afternoon."

"So what would that be?" She felt stupid – not just looking dumb, her expression owlish and slack, slow in thought and deed. As if the world was a talking picture show that was running too slow. "Tell it to me."

"It is very simple. We kill the demon."

"Kill the demon? How?"

"No time for explanations. Once it is over, take your money and get as far away from here as you can because there is something far worse than me on its way."

"How do you know?"

"You don't think the fact that time has stopped is a clue? He's here— Somewhere."

The urge to slap his smug pointy face was hard to resist. *It's like a game with him*, she thought. *Proving six impossible things before breakfast.* She could not remember where the quote came from, some book or other that Jules so adored, but one he quoted often. She looked toward the darkened window. Beyond the dirty glass there were no flashing frames of cables and pipes, nor was the carriage rocking or throbbing as it should when in motion. Time had slowed – stopped – and her brain was running in rhythm, sharpening, clearing. Her understanding flooding back with a vicious snap, the same feeling she had when the "Bennies" Riton occasionally bought for her, crashed her brain into top gear. The sweats and miasmas of a few seconds before had gone in a blinking of one eye.

She spun around to look through the door panel into second class. The crowded space was full of people, but all locked in stasis. A mother stilled in the act of leaning down to wipe her child's mouth; two young women frozen in animated silence; all of the passengers as statues in a variety of poses.

She looked back to Carreau, aghast, but he was gone again. *The bastard has run out on me.*

The doors on the left side of the carriage slid open, letting in a rush of foetid air laden with brake dust and diesel – and a disturbingly familiar figure. She darted forward to grab the canvas cash bag and backed away. As she reversed so Tildmann advanced.

"You have been hard to catch up with." His voice was grating and notably devoid of accent.

"Tildmann." She spat the name out like a bad taste. This man-shaped monster had tried to kill her twice now, and she was very much aware that his achieving a third time lucky result was a distinct possibility.

The creature inclined his head. An oddly formal gesture. "I warned Plourde time and again but would he listen?"

"Where did Etienne go? Rouffignac told me he died in the apartment but I know that can't be true."

"Perhaps he did."

"He wasn't there when I woke. I know that much." She had backed along the carriage as far as she could go. In one hand hung Carreau's canvas bag, and in the other

Pierette's ridiculous parasol and her own purse containing Carreau's gun. She hesitated in calling the sensations he emanated, and washing through her, as "evil" but that was how it felt. Carreau's warning about eyes rattled through her skull like a fire alarm. "There was no one there. I looked."

"I know you did. Your diligence is highly commendable. I thought so at the time."

Tildmann stepped closer, taking his time with all of the arrogance she had come to expect from him. The instinct to stare her enemy down was strong and she struggled to prevent herself succumbing to it. She stared at the brass buttons on his blazer, watching how one of them wobbled with every step, and thinking how it needed re-sewing. It jiggled like a fishing lure – like a target. *Does that make me a fish? The prey?*

Yolanda tightened her grip on the heavier bag, waiting for him to get in range, and swung it as hard and as fast as she was able, connecting with the creature's midriff. She heard his grunt and felt the impact judder up her arm. Dropping the bag she wrenched the gun from her tiny handbag and trained it on the beast. There was only a moment's hesitation before she fired. Once, twice. It was deafening in the confined space of the carriage but the demon's howl was louder still. It lurched toward her. She fired again and ducked away but not fast enough.

A clawed hand grasped at her arm, swinging her around so fast that the weapon flew from her hand to clatter under the seats. Desperation had her bring the parasol around to jab at Tildmann's face – the metal tip skittered off his cheek bone, taking a tight scroll of leathery hide with it. Tildmann released his hold on her, clutching at his face.

Before she could swing the flimsy weapon again he lashed out and caught across her shoulder with a heavy blow. She went down hard, rolling away as far as the seating allowed, scrabbling to rise again, but not before a second blow caught her thigh. There, a few feet where it had slid from her hands, lay the MAB.

Yolanda scrabbled forwards and made a grab. Her leg was grasped and she could only claw at the air a hand span away. She kicked back, feeling the silk of her skirt give way, and cursing violently at the waste. The grip on her leg slackened and she made a desperate dive for the MAB, rolling over and taking aim, her eyes were refusing to focus and her breath came in heaving gasps. She blinked a wellspring of sweat from her eyes and fired a fourth slug in Tildmann's direction.

The demon had already rolled away and she missed.

Both were on their feet before the sound had died.

All pretence of humanity fell away and Yolanda was gazing at a visage that was both terrible and beautiful. Like Tildmann and yet not. Gone was the duelling scar and military hair cut. His skin now was a luminous white and his eyes vivid red. Her head swam and she remembered to look away from those ruddy eyes.

"What are you, really?" she asked. "Was it you in Plourde's apartment? I saw something else there. And in the cemetery. Carreau told me it was you but—" She gestured with the gun in his direction, taking a briefest glance through to the far carriage and seeing all remained in stasis. Playing for time seemed ludicrous but it was all she had, given Carreau's desertion. "This wasn't it. I saw a … a creature. A monster."

"You would prefer to fight me in that guise?" He shuddered momentarily and the scaly creature she had seen in the cemetery park stood before her.

She swallowed hard, gulping down her fear along with a spoonful of bile. A small chink of hope lay in the dark patches pooling around the creature's feet. At least one of her shots had hit its target, and hit well if the quantity of life's liquid spreading around was a clue. It explained why she had not been attacked with more ferocity. "So you shape change? Like Carreau?" she said.

A snort of derisions escaped the rubbery lips. "A mangy dog?"

"It serves him well enough. He is Loup Garou – what else would he need to be?"

"His kind are nothing," Tildmann grunted and swayed on his feet.

Yolanda could empathise. Her own head was less than clear. The scent of his blood itched in her sinuses. Not merely metallic, more acid. *Ichor*, she wondered, *is that the right word*? He was breathing raggedly, catching on the intake and gurgling on the out. And another sound. Further up the carriage. A snuffling or scuffling, a distraction. She shut it out. "He is skilled enough to have survived a very long time."

"Oh yes, he survives. Usually by throwing his compatriots to the sharks. Or innocent bystanders, like your Jules."

"I— What does that mean?"

"Jules died of a fever."

"Yes," she said.

"Like the one you have now? Ever since that junk yard mongrel sank his teeth into you? Did Jules get bitten, my dear?"

She cast her mind back, recalling the bandage on her husband's arm that he had refused to explain. What was Tildmann trying to say? For a moment she forgot herself and looked into his eyes. Her senses blackened and she staggered against a seating bar, jarring her mind into the world. "He said it was an accident."

"It always is. Some are lucky and cross over easily, others, the ones who fight it most, they die."

Tildmann continued, edging ever closer, and Yolanda ever back.

"I will not believe that. He had no choice about how he died," she said.

"And you have?"

A shrug. "Perhaps. Do you?"

"I am not the one bleeding to death." She waved at the pool around his feet.

"Survival is a given."

"Immortal?"

"We … transform. Oh, the base form remains but our earthly body—" Tildmann's features returned. "This one I came across on Flanders field," he said. "It has served its purpose. I could be you next." Tildmann shook more violently and without warning was gone – and Yolanda was staring now … at herself. Apparently perfect in all detail from white hat to chic heels, except there was no sign of injuries. No bleeding. No bandaged hand.

He – she – it ventured a step forward.

Yolanda took aim as a white swirl of unconsciousness made her stagger to her right. Blinking it away, she lined up the weapon once more, her finger tightening on the trigger. Along the length of her arm, and the MAB's short snout, she took a bead on her own body, and hesitated still. She had killed before but shooting herself was not something she had ever thought to do. It was an unnatural act. Is *that me? Or is she – it – a replica? If I shoot that image will I die?* Indecision and doubt built rapidly whilst she stared into her own eyes. Tildmann's eyes.

The flash of something to her left and a tug at her arm broke the contact. She let rip with the MAB and heard the howl. She fired again and her mind was cleared, as though a switch had been pulled.

Her doppelgänger slumped into the corner seat, a heavy wooden knife handle protruding from her neck. There was blood enough now. Gouts of dazzling, sticky, redness, turning rapidly brown as it was sucked greedily into the green silk of the suit.

Yolanda blinked hard against the world that was blurring once again, distorting, wavering. As she dropped to the floor, the grit and shit grinding into her hands and knees, the carriage doors closed. Crouching between the seats, feeling the thrum of motors vibrating the hard surface, she was aware of a warmth beside her that was comforting, as time reasserted its hold on the world.

The train swayed into the station of Porte Dorée and the doors re-opened onto a bustling platform and its thick curtain of sound. Then, above the melee, a fresh scream, emanating from a group of travellers, entered the train, reverberated through the carriage and back, across the station concourse. A young woman shrinking back from the sight of the beautiful body clad in green silk that was slipping to the floor.

A shout. A male voice calling for someone to "fetch le

Gendarme".

Within moments the platform was awash with people, pouring from carriages and corridors, craning for a glimpse of a dying woman with the obscene knife hilt protruding from her neck, dead in all but name, though her lips still moved around half-formed and silent syllables.

Not one of them noticed the pair of dogs slink out from under the seats and trot quickly along the darker edge of the platform and up the steps onto a wet street glistening in the sun.

~~~

Author's Note

The *Métro Murder* is one of the most famous unsolved crimes of the 1930s. Who was Laetitia Toureaux? What were her links within the murky world of spies and secret political movements? All of those things remain shrouded in mystery, despite the fact that her movements on her final day are well documented. How was she stabbed to death in an apparently empty Métro carriage? And by whom? This story offers one potential solution.

Also by Jan Edwards

Winter Downs

by

Jan Edwards

Winner of the Arnold Bennett Book Prize!

Bunch Courtney stumbles upon the body of Jonathan Frampton in a woodland clearing. Is this a case of suicide, or is it murder? Bunch is determined to discover the truth but can she persuade the dour Chief Inspector Wright to take her seriously?

In January of 1940 a small rural community on the Sussex Downs, already preparing for invasion from across the Channel, finds itself deep in the grip of a snowy landscape, with an ice-cold killer on the loose.

Available from Penkhull Press

In Her Defence

by

Jan Edwards

Bunch Courtney's hopes for a quiet market-day lunch with her sister are shattered when a Dutch refugee dies a horribly painful death before their eyes. A few days later Bunch receives a letter from her old friend Cecile saying that her father, Professor Benoir, has been murdered in an eerily similar fashion.

Two deaths by poisoning in a single week. Co-incidence? Bunch does not believe that any more than Chief Inspector William Wright.

Set against a backdrop of escalating war and the massed internments of 1940, the pair are drawn together in a race to prevent the murderer from striking again.

Available from Penkhull Press

Sussex Tales

by

Jan Edwards

Winner of the Winchester Conference Slim Volume prize. Jan Edwards' prize-winning *Sussex Tales* runs a witty and thought-provoking gamut of village events and of its more curious characters.

From fanged ferrets to bulls in lead masks; ancient hand grenades to exploding ginger beer; cricketing dogs to wassailing orchards, *Sussex Tales* weaves traditional country wines and recipes, folklore and local dialect, into stories of a farming childhood in the vanished world of 1950s and 60s rural life.

"Superbly crafted ... creating sub-plots as it unfolds with purpose and fluidity... Whether you're from Sussex or not, this is an appealing and often amusing collection of tales from a bygone age. I defy you not to like them." – Barry Lillie

Available from Penkhull Press

Leinster Gardens
and Other Subtleties

Fourteen ghost stories by Jan Edwards

Includes: Concerning Events at Leinster Gardens. He handed the maid his hat and replaced it with a coronet of silk holly leaves and tinsel. She gave him only the smallest raise of an eyebrow. "Ghost of Christmas Present," he said...

The Waiting. She picked up the hem of her nightdress and ran the length of the gallery. She wanted to race them to the door, to greet her father. Why, then, did a tiny part of her hesitate? Why should she be afraid? From the landing she heard the doors of the great hall being flung open...

From the introduction: "...Ghost stories, adeptly told, often with a sense of locale and time neatly placed within the narratives. Her family history informs and inspires some of her stories. Folklore figures as a focus in more than one story, whether urban myth or historical lore. But ghostly they are and deceptively disturbing."

Available from The Alchemy Press

Fables and Fabrications

by

Jan Edwards

From the arctic wastes of Norway to a fun-laden evening at the fair, Jan Edwards leads us through a world where nothing is as it seems. Shape changers and ancient spirits roam, and cats play their inscrutable parts in stories that unsettle and disturb the reader's perceptions.

Fourteen tales of mystery, mirth and the macabre. Chosen from her back catalogue of horror and dark fantasy, these stories, leavened with a sprinkle of verse, have been collected for the first time in this volume.

"Jan Edwards has yet to let me down" – Dave Brzeski, British Fantasy Society

"A really good story made brilliant by the final reveal" – Jim Macleod, Ginger Nuts of Horror

Available from Penkhull Press

www.ingramcontent.com/pod-product-compliance
Lightning Source LLC
Chambersburg PA
CBHW021935170626
46807CB00007B/3119